TIMMY FAILURE

THE BOOK YOU'RE NOT SUPPOSED TO HAVE

Praise for the series

"This inspired book will prompt outbursts of laughter."
The Sunday Times 100 Children's Modern Classics

"A fabulously fun read ... original and quirky, with real heart."
Philip Ardagh, *Guardian*

"For T...   ...ss
is ...

Lincoln P...   ...Nate

"Will gl...   ...ke
cheese...   ..."
Adam, aged...   ...s.co.uk

"A bri...   ..."
...

"If you are a fan of *Diary of a Wimpy Kid* or *Tom Gates* you will be a fan of this series."
Alice, aged 9, *Lovereading4kids.co.uk*

"Seldom has failure been so likable—or so funny."
The Wall Street Journal

TIMMY FAILURE

THE BOOK YOU'RE NOT SUPPOSED TO HAVE

Stephan Pastis

WALKER
BOOKS

First published in Great Britain 2016 by Walker Books Ltd
87 Vauxhall Walk, London SE11 5HJ

This edition published 2019

2 4 6 8 10 9 7 5 3 1

This book has been typeset in Nimrod

Printed and bound by CPI Group (UK) Ltd, Croydon CR0 4YY

British Library Cataloguing in Publication Data:
a catalogue record for this book is available from the British Library

ISBN 978-1-4063-8722-3

www.walker.co.uk

www.timmyfailure.com

Author's Note:
From the Desk of
Timmy Failure

This book was not meant for publication. It is a private record of a sensitive time in my life as a detective.

And then the manuscript was stolen. Which is how it ended up in your hands.

So please put the book down and stop reading.

Preface:
Oh, Look, You're Still Reading

I don't know much about you.

But I do know this:

You don't have a lot of respect for an Author's Note.

Because when the Author's Note on the previous page asked you to put this book down and stop reading, you took that to mean:

So let me get right to the point.

I am Timmy Failure. I am a detective.

And I am banned from detective work.

BANNED

You don't need to know the details.

You just need to know that none of the

detective work you are about to read about was supposed to happen.

And the only reason I kept a record of it at all was that I knew I was going through the most productive career phase ever experienced by a detective.

So if you're going to keep reading (and so far, I haven't been able to stop you), I need you to raise your right hand and swear the following oath:

I, (state your name), do hereby agree to never reveal the contents of this book to anyone, including, but not limited to, Timmy's mother, who would crush Timmy like a bug if she ever found out he was doing detective work during the time of his banishment.

And I do hereby further agree that if any part of this oath shall be broken by me, intentionally or otherwise, I shall be subjected to the following punishment:

*I will be covered in mustard and
eaten by a polar bear.*

CHAPTER
1

Not Really the Start of the Story, but Intriguing Nonetheless

I am Hawaii Joe.

And my sunglasses are large.

As is my polar bear.

Whom I have named after the state fish of Hawaii:

Humuhumunukunukuapuaa.

"Come here, Humuhumunukunukuapuaa," I say to my polar bear. "Because I am about to make an announcement to all of the employees of our detective agency."

(Well, it is not really *our* detective agency. It is *my* detective agency. But I like to be inclusive so as not to offend the feelings of Humuhumunukunukuapuaa.)

So I press the red intercom button on my telephone.

"Greetings, employees of Failure, Inc. This is your founder, president, and CEO, joined by my administrative assistant, Humuhumunukunukuapuaa."

As I talk, I see my employees begin to gather outside the glass wall of my office.

"It is hard to imagine, but it was not long ago that I, Timmy Failure, was doubted by the petty masses, including my rotund best friend, Rollo Tookus; my tangerine-scented classmate, Molly Moskins; and my lifelong foe, She Whose Name Shall Not Be Uttered But Can Now Be Uttered Because We Have Defeated Her and No Longer Care, Corrina Corrina."

There is a roar of approval from the employees.

"But those days are a distant memory. And now look at us. We are a massive detective agency with over a hundred employees, multiple offices, a global reach, and free donuts every Friday."

Everyone applauds.

"Speaking of the donuts, I understand there has been a battle going on for the maple bar ones."

Humuhumunukunukuapuaa nods.

"My administrative assistant here informs me that some of you have been seen racing to the donut box and licking the maple bar donuts so as to claim them as your own."

A few of the employees look away.

"I am speaking specifically of Liz Bicknell, Carter Hasegawa, and Ann Stott. Please stop licking the maple bar donuts."

Heads down, Liz, Carter, and Ann leave the group of gathered employees in shame.

"Now some of you are probably wondering how we got here. How I took my grand vision of a detective empire and made it reality."

Humuhumunukunukuapuaa coughs.

"How *we* made it reality," I say, correcting myself.

Humuhumunukunukuapuaa smiles.

"We did it by following one guiding moral principle. A principle that I have had printed upon a banner that will now hang in our office forevermore. And it is this:"

CHAPTER
2
Ship of Fools

"You are not doing any detective work," says my mother.

"For how long?" I ask.

"I told you already."

"But you said six months."

"And that's what I meant."

"But *six months*? You'll destroy the agency!"

"We're not going to keep having this discussion, Timmy."

"But the punishment doesn't fit the crime."

"You ran away from home!"

"I chased a felon across state lines!"[1]

---

1. All the details of this event are contained in *Timmy Failure 4: Sanitized for Your Protection*, a modern-day classic of literature.

"Enough, Timmy," she says, taking a meat loaf out of the oven. "Besides, this will give you more time to concentrate on your schoolwork, and maybe do some other things."

"What other things?" I mutter, suspicious of my mother, her tone, and her meat loaf.

"I signed you up for piano lessons."

"You what?" I cry. "You just said I needed more time for my schoolwork!"

"And you'll have it. Giving up your detective work frees up all that time and more."

"Oh, my God," I mutter, staggering backward like a drunken sailor.

Drunken sailor

"And besides," adds my mother, "I saw you trying to play the piano when we were at Aunt Colander's house. You seemed to enjoy it."

"What are you—a spy?" I shout.

"Nope," she answers.

"So I guess you saw me help her gardener make his tapioca sculptures out of the bushes. Did you sign me up for tapioca lessons, too?"

"Topiary," she says. "Tapioca is a pudding. And that reminds me. . . ." She reaches into the fridge and pulls out a bowl of jelly. "Tonight's dessert."

"I don't want it," I say. "My life's sail is in tatters."

"Oh, Timmy," she says, kneeling down to put her arms around me. "Don't you think you're being a little dramatic?"

"No. You're destroying my business," I reply.

"Okay," she says. "How 'bout I make you a proposition?"

"Good. I think we studied those in class."

"You studied prepositions, not propositions."

"Please stop correcting me," I answer. "I know what I studied."

"Fine," says my mother. "Then I'll make you a deal."

"What kind of deal?"

"A fair one."

"Okay. But I'll have to run it by my

lawyer. And my accountant, too. He can be very aggressive."

Aggressive accountant

My mom smiles. "If you promise me you'll do your best with school and with your piano lessons, maybe I'll cut your detective ban a little short."

"How short?"

"When is the last day of school?" she asks.

"In 37 days, 18 hours, and 24 minutes," I answer.

Not that I was counting.

"That's a bit sooner than I thought," my mother says. "But okay, the ban will end then. *IF* you do what I say."

I hug my mother's leg like it is a ship's mast in a tempest.

"Now let go of my leg so I can put raisins on the pudding."

"Raisins?" I say. "I loathe raisins."

"They're not for you," she says. "They're for Larry and Merry."

And hearing those names, I am cast into the rolling sea.

CHAPTER 3

Something About Merry and Larry

This one's Larry.

Larry

She is a loon.

And she needs to be placed in a home.

The other one is Merry.

She is Larry's sister.

Merry's name is spelled that way because she was born on Christmas Day.

But don't let the name fool you.

For she is not merry.

Merry (not merry)

Merry and Larry are my cousins. They are staying with us until the middle of summer.

Merry has one of the twin beds in my bedroom. Larry has the other. And I'm in the narrow gorge between them.

Which I call Death Valley.

DEATH VALLEY

And Death Valley has entailed a certain loss of privacy.

So now I'm in a Mr. Froggie pop-up tent.

But I don't think there will be three of us for long.

Because Larry is a homicidal maniac.

And soon she will try to kill me.

CHAPTER 4

Sing Us a Song, You're the Timmy Man

If Larry doesn't do me in, the Buppy Guppy will.

The Buppy Guppy is part of the Beginning Piano songbook series. And Ms. Hardie-Heeron insists I learn the first song.

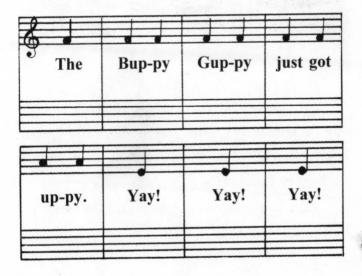

Ms. Hardie-Heeron is my piano teacher. She is old.

And she loves the Buppy Guppy.

My mom hired Ms. Hardie-Heeron because she is the only piano teacher in the neighborhood who does the lesson at *your* house, instead of her house.

And that was one less place my mother had to drive me.

So my mother rented an upright piano and every day I am supposed to practice it for half an hour. Here is how much I have practiced so far:

This does not please Ms. Hardie-Heeron, who sees me as an ungovernable ne'er-do-well. Which is understandable, given how little she knows about the harried life of a detective. A life that has little room for the Buppy Guppy.

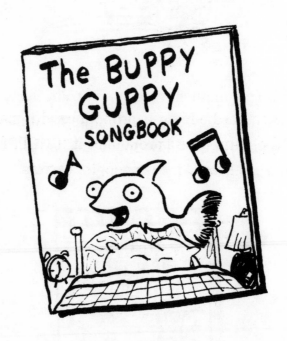

So for inspiration, Ms. Hardie-Heeron has brought me a tiny plastic bust of some composer named Frédéric Chopin.

This guy →

CHOPIN

Ms. Hardie-Heeron pronounces his name "SHOW-pann." But I pronounce it "CHOPPin'," as in the phrase "I was choppin' carrots."

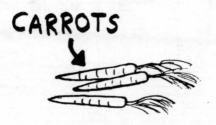

CARROTS

And I do not like the way Choppin' Carrots judges me for not practicing. So when I walk by the piano, I poke him in the eye.

And I especially did not like the way he looked at me when I rewrote the words to the Buppy Guppy.

CHAPTER
5

There Is No Joy in Rollo, the Mighty Teachers Have Struck Out

I awaken to a telephone call.

And it is the most glorious news that a human being can ever hear.

"All of the teachers went on strike," says my best friend, Rollo Tookus. "So there's no school until they come back."

The news is so momentous that I rush to his house to hear it in person.

Bearing gifts.

"What's that thing?" Rollo asks, pointing to the object I am holding on his porch.

"Champagne," I answer. "We're going to celebrate."

"We can't drink that," answers Rollo.

"I know, but we can pop the cork and spray each other. Like professionals."

I pop the cork. It strikes me in the cranium.

THWACK

"My precious bean!" I cry as I fall to the ground. "Good-bye, cruel world."

"You're fine," says the rotund Rollo, who is never right but often thinks he is.

So perhaps now, just before my demise, would be a good time to discuss Rollo.

Charles "Rollo" Tookus is my best friend.

He is big-boned.

And he has an unhealthy obsession with grades.

Thus, his grade point average is 4.2. As mine would be if I were obsessed by something as mundane as grades.

And concern about grades is not his only

flaw. Because Rollo Tookus also has a profound inability to seize the moment.

"I don't think the teachers' strike is a good thing," says Rollo. "I don't want them to be gone."

"What?" I shout from the ground. "I thought the cork struck *me* in the bean. But it must have struck you. Because nonsense is streaming forth from your head."

"I like school," he says.

"Did you *drink* the champagne?" I ask.

"I'm not drunk, Timmy. I just enjoy school."

And sadly, I know that it's true.

For every day, Rollo Tookus arrives at school at precisely 6:00 a.m., two hours before the first bell. And well before most roosters greet the dawn.

And his arrival at 6:00 a.m. is as dependable as the upcoming sunrise.

So dependable, in fact, that the keepers of the world's official time zones depend on Rollo's arrival at school to set their watches.

And it is so early that the school doors are still locked. So Rollo sits outside, and surrounded by sleeping roosters, he studies.

But while it is one thing to arrive at school early, it's another to brag about liking the place.

So as Rollo begins praising school, I cover his mouth before someone overhears him and puts us both in the loony bin.

"Listen to me," I say to Rollo. "Because right now you are spouting madness. A teachers' strike means no school. And no school means freedom. And freedom means doing whatever the heck we want. Now maybe for you that means something ludicrous, like more studying. But for me, it means getting my business going again."

"Your detective business?"

"Of course my detective business."

"But didn't your mom say you couldn't do that?"

"Yes, but that was before the teachers' strike. So we have what is known as an unforeseeable circumstance. Which, according to my lawyer, renders my agreement with my mother kaput."

"That's not a legal term, Timmy."

"You know nothing about the law, Rollo Tookus."

"I know your mom would ground you for life. Or maybe longer."

"Sure," I answer. "If she found out. But she's not going to. Because my detective office will be here. In your house."

"Oh, no, it won't," cries Rollo, his round head beginning to shake nervously. "I don't want anything to do with this."

"Well, I can't put it where I live," I say.

"What's wrong with where you live?"

"It has a Merry and a Larry."

"Your cousins?" asks Rollo.

"Yes, my cousins. They're staying with us. And there's not a square inch of privacy, much less room for a covert detective office."

"Good. You're not supposed to be doing any detective work anyway."

"But you, on the other hand . . ." I add, ignoring Rollo's warning. "*You* have a spare bedroom in your house."

I point to his house.

Rollo runs inside and locks the door.

"Open this door," I say to Rollo Tookus, pounding on the door with my fist.

"I can't hear you," he says from behind the door. "Reading."

I bang on the door with my head, for greater emphasis.

"Still reading," says Rollo.

"You cannot live your life in fear!" I yell through the closed door.

"Yes, I can," he answers.

"I'll be back!" I cry, hair mussed but spirit defiant.

So I pick up the empty champagne bottle and walk down his driveway to the sidewalk.

Where I run into Ms. Hardie-Heeron.

CHAPTER
6
Every Rose Has Its Thorny Cousin

Ms. Hardie-Heeron will no longer be coming to our house.

She says the drive is too far.

Which was her diplomatic way of getting rid of this pupil:

That should have ended the failed piano experiment right there.

But my mother didn't get the hint.

So now she says I have to go to Ms. Hardie-Heeron's house for my lessons.

But it's too far to walk. And my mother can't drive me because of her job.

And that should have definitely ended the failed piano experiment.

But no. Not when your mother is as unyielding as a brick wall.

MOM   BRICK WALL

So now she says I have to ride a bike.

But I don't ride bikes.

And that should have buried this failed piano experiment right in the ground.

But no. It will be *me* getting buried in the ground.

Because this is who will teach me how to ride a bike:

That's right. Doctor Death herself. The Grim Reaper. The Doomsdame.

And thus, my life is near its end.

So the question now is not *whether* she will kill me, but *how*.

Perhaps it will be the collective impact of all these falls. Death by a thousand cuts.

Or perhaps she is waiting for the day that I can comfortably ride this evil bicycle. At which point she will send me on a questionable bike route.

And that day may be closer. Because today I rode unassisted across the entire length of our apartment building's parking lot.

And straight toward the rose garden that lines the perimeter.

Unaware of how one stops.

But learning that this is one way:

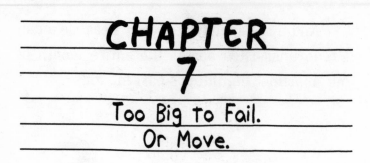

CHAPTER 7

Too Big To Fail.
Or Move.

I am on my mother's cell phone talking to her boyfriend, Doorman Dave. And I am calmly recounting the story of the Great Bicycle Tragedy.

"I was stabbed a thousand times!" I shout. "The girl is homicidal."

My mother leans in to the cell phone. "He fell into some rosebushes, Dave. His cousin Larry is teaching him how to ride a bike."

"And I'm missing a tooth!" I shout.

Missing tooth

My mother shakes her head.

"And the apartment complex suffered irreparable damage," I add. "I think they may have to tear it down."

"That's terrible," says Doorman Dave.

DOORMAN DAVE

My mother grabs the phone out of my hands. "It wasn't a permanent tooth, Dave. And all they broke was a sprinkler head."

I lean over my mother's shoulder with an addendum. "So, Dave, with all that's going on, and my recovery time uncertain, we won't be joining you in Chicago. Good luck, be well, and Godspeed."

My mother frowns and walks off with the phone to talk to Dave alone. In her bedroom. As she does every night.

The two of them are getting married in the summer. And then we may move. Or we may not. But I don't care.

Because by then, I will have built my

detective business up to unprecedented heights.

And there will be no way I can uproot it.

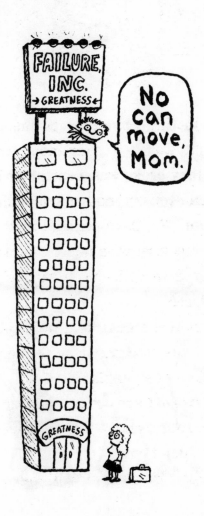

CHAPTER
8
Substi-Toots

There will be no building my business up to *any* height.

Because school is back in session.

Not because the teachers have returned.

But because the school has hired substitute teachers.

And ours is "Toots."

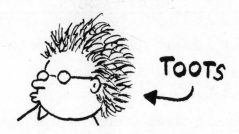

I do not know who Toots is. Or what lagoon the school found her in. But I do know she wants to be called Toots.

And that is about all she has taught us.

Because the only other thing she has done is sit at the back of the class and eat jelly beans.

Toots eats them by the fistful. And the only time she looks up is when someone does something wrong. In which case, she stands up, and, with jelly beans falling out of her mouth, says, "Behave. Or I'll send you to Dark Caverns."

Now I do not know what Dark Caverns is. But I sense Toots is from there.

So I don't want to go.

But the bigger punishment is just seeing Toots stand. Because her trousers are pulled up almost to her ears.

Perhaps that's how they wear trousers in Dark Caverns. Or perhaps her trousers are bulletproof, and she wants to protect her vital organs.

PING
PING

Whichever it is, those of us in Toots's class are left with nothing to do.

And thus each student must forge his or her own academic path.

So Rollo reads ahead in the textbook.

Molly Moskins decorates the room.

Nunzio Benedici shoves stolen jelly beans up his nose.

Angel de Manzanas Naranjas sets fire to his shoe.

And Corrina Corrina writes private and discreet things in her journal.

Which I read.

I used to be at war with Corrina Corrina. But that was when she was in the detective business.

But then she retired. Because she could not compete with me.

And I am nothing if not a gracious winner.

But the business of winning will not continue if my detective business is out of business.

So I am thinking about turning the lemon that is school into lemonade by building a detective office here, in the classroom.

Which I begin to accomplish by reassembling some desks.

Until I get resistance.

CHAPTER
9
Merry, Merry,
Quite Contrary

I am not going to Dark Caverns.

But I am going to Home Despot.

That's the giant hardware store in our town. While we once had a lot of little hardware stores, we now have just one big one. And it's the biggest place I've ever seen.

I'm here because we need to replace the sprinkler head we broke in the Great Bicycle Tragedy.

THIS
→

And since my mother couldn't take me to Home Despot, she asked my cousin Merry to do it.

MERRY

Merry is different from her sister, Larry.

For one thing, she has a driver's license.

And for another thing, she's not a homicidal maniac.

Though I probably wouldn't know if she were. Because she never says a word.

Until we're halfway to the hardware store. And she says this:

"Do you love others, Timothy?"

Her sudden speech rattles the air like a cannon in a monastery.

So I am momentarily stunned.

"Do you?" she asks again.

I remain silent.

"You're not answering," she says again.

So I resort to a classic detective maneuver.

And turn the question around on her.

"I dunno. Do you?"

"I do," she says. "I love everyone and everything. Trees. Dogs. Rainbows. Ponies."

I quickly wish I hadn't asked.

"Mother Nature. Father Time. Babies' smiles. Subway tiles."

Suddenly, she is rhyming like Dr. Seuss.

I contemplate rolling down the window and jumping from the moving vehicle.

But then the car stops. And mercifully, we are at Home Despot.

And my cousin turns to me.

"And you should love others, too, Timothy."

Then she smiles.

And it is deeply unsettling.

And using my natural instincts as a detective, I realize that Merry and Larry are not relatives.

They are escapees from an insane asylum.

Or maybe they are both. Relatives AND escapees.

Which causes me to make a profound philosophical note in my detective log:

So as we walk through the garden section that Home Despot keeps in its parking lot, I keep a line of sturdy garden gnomes between me and Merry.

And in doing so, I run smack into my destiny.

CHAPTER 10

Getting Out of Dodge

"What did you run into?" asks Rollo Tookus. "A garden gnome?"

It is lunch hour and we are waiting to be divided into two dodgeball teams.

"I'll tell you that part of the story later," I explain. "Right now I need to focus."

"Focus on what?"

"Focus on being on the right dodgeball team. To give myself the greatest chance of protecting my cranium."

"You don't have a choice. Angel and Scutaro are the captains."

"So?"

"So they pick who they want," says Rollo.

"Well, that's a stupid system. Who thought up that?"

But I know who thought up that.

Toots.

For while she may be sloth-like in class, she is a burst of energy on the playground.

Where, high on sugar, she plays dodgeball with reckless abandon.

Her overzealous participation in such a violent activity surely violates a number of federal and state laws. But with the real teachers on strike, the school is now in chaos.

And the prisoners are running the joint.

"I'll take Nunzio," says the oversized Angel.

"I'll take Corrina Corrina," says the ratlike Scutaro.

Oversized Angel

Ratlike Scutaro

"Then I guess I'll take Molly," says Angel.

"And I guess I'll pick Toody Tululu," says Scutaro.

The teams mostly chosen, only Rollo and I are left.

And the two of us stand alone at the edge of the playground.

"I suppose I gotta have Rollo," says Angel. "But he's gonna be pretty easy to hit." Rollo pauses and lumbers toward Angel's team.

And I stand by myself at the edge of the playground.

"Oh, no," I say. "I see what is happening."

Both team captains stare at me.

"You've both taken too many dodgeballs to the head," I explain. "And now you can't think straight. Up is down. Black is white. Last is first. And the first shall be last."

I point toward our substitute teacher.

"Toots, start the selection process over. And this time *I'll* pick the teams."

And as I say it, I am struck by half a dozen dodgeballs.

WHAM BAM WHAM
BAM
WHAM BAM

All thrown by my fellow students.
And I can't report them to Toots.
Because she threw one, too.

CHAPTER 11

The Chapter Before the Chapter Before the Chapter in Which You Finally Find Out What I Discovered in the Home Despot Parking Lot

I know you want to know what it is I found in the Home Despot parking lot.

But as you saw, I was struck in the bean by a number of dodgeballs.

And as a result, I have forgotten what I was going to say.

CHAPTER
12

The Chapter Before the Chapter in Which You Finally Find Out What I Discovered in the Home Despot Parking Lot

Okay.

Now I remember.

But before I tell you, I need to go over something one more time.

And that is this:

My mother cannot know this part.

Seriously.

My mother cannot know this part.

So if you are reading this book somewhere where *your* mother can see it, there is always the possibility that your mother will read it and tell my mother everything.

Because mothers have what is known as the Mother Hotline. Which is a special phone line connecting them to every other mother in the world.

THE MOTHER HOTLINE

Dads do not have such a thing. Dads only have what is known as a regular phone.

So before we go any further, I'm going to have to ask that you take precautions to prevent your mother from seeing the next chapter.

These precautions will (1) ensure that your mother cannot physically see the chapter and (2) be discreet enough that they do not draw attention to you.

There are three possible precautions you can take.

PRECAUTION NUMBER ONE:

Sit in your bedroom covered by a cluster of open umbrellas.

If your mother asks you what you are doing, say this:

EXPECTING RAIN, MA.

PRECAUTION NUMBER TWO:

Purchase the head from one of the costumed characters at your nearby amusement park and wear it as you read. The head will be roomy enough to accommodate your own head AND the book. Thus, your mother will have no idea what you are doing in there.

But if your mother *does* ask you what you are doing, say this:

MOTHER, I'VE CHANGED.

But if for some reason Precaution Number Two is not practical, there is always Precaution Number Three.

PRECAUTION NUMBER THREE:

Send your mother to a moose farm.

CHAPTER 13

The Chapter in Which You Finally Find Out What I Discovered in the Home Despot Parking Lot. Which Is This:

Garden sheds.

CHAPTER 14

Shedding My Problems

The last chapter was short on details.

So let me add some.

ARE YOU STILL UNDER YOUR UMBRELLAS?

The Home Despot has a massive selection of garden sheds. They are small little rooms suited for the storage of

1. garden tools;
2. cow manure; and
3. the world's greatest detective.

And they are roomy enough to fit the detective's administrative assistant. Provided that the assistant can remember to duck and not hit his head for the fiftieth time.

Best of all, there are dozens of these sheds scattered throughout the Home Despot parking lot. And there is no way any Home Despot employee can monitor the interior of that many sheds.

Added to all this is the fact that I no longer need Merry to drive me here.

Because I now have my own mode of transportation.

Given to me by her sister, Larry.

Who, due to her criminal role in the Great

Bicycle Tragedy, felt obligated to provide me with a new mode of transportation.

And it is significantly more stable than the last.

Larry got the tricycle from a promotional event at her new job. A place in the mall called Tri-Cities Undergarments.

And thus it comes with a flag I cannot remove.

Cyclops Killer,
Run Run Away

But the tricycle is not the only legacy of the Great Bicycle Tragedy.

For there is also my missing tooth.

And my mother is worried about its effect on my smile. Which is odd because detectives don't smile.

Not even for school photos.

Which is why my last one looked like this:

That's a grimace. And it's very detective-like.

As is self-promotion. Which was my school photo the year before.

FAILURE, INC.
FOR ALL YOUR DETECTIVE NEEDS

But it was my most detective-like act of all that finally pushed my mom over the edge and stopped her from ever ordering any more school photos.

And that was the year I went undercover.

And yet for some reason my mother is still worried about my smile.

And it is for that reason that I am here:

Apparently the dentist who looked at my missing tooth noticed that my other teeth were crooked. And so he said we had to go to an orthodontist. Who, according to my mom, is a nice man that straightens your teeth.

Which explains everything but the presence of the girl on the right:

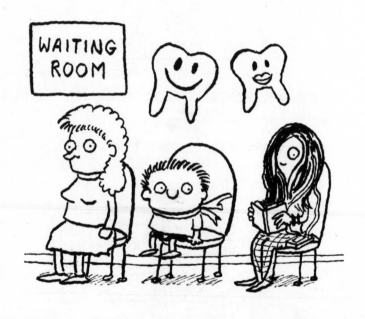

"What's *she* doing here?" I whisper to my mom. Though whispering isn't necessary given the volume of music emanating from Larry's headphones.

"The mall she works at is just down the street. So I told her I'd drop her off after your appointment."

"That's generous of you. Did you know that Larry is a serial killer?"

"Timmy, stop."

"She can't hear me."

"I don't care. You're being silly."

"Silly?" I retort, gap-toothed, from atop the waiting-room chair.

"Sit down," says my mother.

So I sit back down.

"Fine," I tell my mother. "Ignore the signs."

"And what signs are those?" my mother says, leafing through a magazine.

"First off, her name is Larry."

"Her real name is Lauren. And that's how she likes to shorten it."

"HA!" I exclaim.

"Quiet, Timmy. She's sitting right there."

So I lean into my mother's ear and whisper, "She changed her name because she's running from the authorities."

My mother stares at me. "Are you sure *you're* not running from the authorities?"

"This is no time for humor," I answer, dismissing my mother's attempt at levity.

"Yeah, well, you're being pretty funny," answers my mom. "So please, tell me all the other warning signs."

"Okay," I answer. "She has one eye. Like the Cyclops."

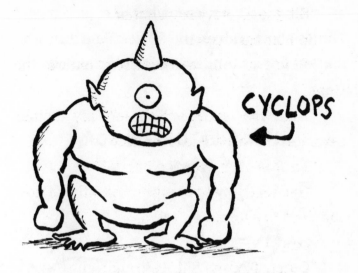

CYCLOPS

"She has two eyes, Timmy. One is covered by her hair."

"Well, she has tight trousers."

"So?" asks my mother.

"So they cut circulation to the brain, leaving her with only her animal instincts."

"Okay, Timmy, I'm gonna read my magazine now."

"And that's another thing!" I shout.

"Keep your voice down," says my mother.

So I whisper into my mother's ear.

"Have you noticed what the girl *reads*? Things about wolves and fairies. And unicorns that eat horses. And horses that eat unicorns."

HORSE EATING UNICORN

"They're called fantasy novels, Timmy. And I don't think the horses eat unicorns."

"You bet they do. Unless they're stopped by the tiny people. The hairy ones with the pointy ears."

"Okay," says my mother. "I think this conversation is over."

"Fine. But the books aren't healthy," I answer. "Certainly not for Scary Larry. I mean, really—I've never met anyone more menacing."

Until that moment.

When I meet someone more menacing.

CHAPTER
16
Goni with the Wind

"Hello, big guy!" says the tall man with the fake glasses and fake moustache. "I'm Dr. Alfredo Goni. Your orthodontist."

"Why are you wearing that?" I ask.

"Because I'm fun! And I like my patients to know that orthodontics can be fun!"

As he says that, I hear a drill, followed by a muffled cry.

"Exactly what kind of operation are you running here?" I ask.

"I'm sorry," my mother says to Dr. Goni.

"Hold on, Mother," I say, and then turn back to the strange man. "*I'm* not sorry," I tell him. "Because I know something my mother does not. Which is that only spies wear disguises."

"Dr. Goni," says my mother, "my son can be a little—"

I hear another drill.

"Good God. He's torturing people for information," I say to my mother. "It's a massive counterintelligence operation."

My mother slaps her hand over my mouth.

Dr. Goni smiles and pulls a plush doll shaped like a tooth from behind his back.

"Did you hear that, Mickey Molar? He thinks we're spies!"

"What's that you say?" he says to Mickey Molar. "You want to go home with Timmy?"

He hands me the doll.

And I tear Mickey Molar to shreds.

"Timmy!" yells my mother. "What in the world do you think—?"

"He's buried a microphone in this thing! It's an intelligence tool! I'll prove it to you!"

I continue ripping Mickey Molar apart until there is no more Mickey Molar.

And no microphone that I can find.

"This isn't over," I say to him.

But it is.

Because we're asked to leave.

CHAPTER 17

All You Need Is Merry

"You probably shouldn't have ripped up the doll," says Doorman Dave to me over the phone. "I think your mother's pretty upset."

"Orthodontists need to be stopped, Dave. They're not good people."

"Well, it wasn't polite."

"Uh, Dave," I answer. "First off, these are stressful times. There's a Merry, a Larry, a missing tooth, and a teachers' strike that is crippling my academic future. Secondly, you're Doorman Dave. And you don't get to decide punishments."

As I say it, I hear Merry walk past me on her way to the kitchen. She grabs a pad of paper from near the phone and writes a note to me, underlining the words with such force that she almost tears through the page.

So I write a note back.

CHAPTER
18

A Day in the Life (of a
Detective Whose Office
Just So Happens to Be in a
Home Despot Parking Lot)

I read the news today.

It said that due to the continuing teachers'
strike, the school is running out of money to
pay for substitute teachers. So school is being
reduced to half days.

And not everyone is ecstatic.

Pleased with this development, I use the extra time to commute to work early.

Stared at by adoring fans.

But business at the office is slow. So my assistant and I pass the time just staring out the window of our global headquarters.

I could increase business through proper signage and television advertising.

But my mother would find out.

SO COME TO FAILURE, INC.... NOW IN THE HOME DESPOT PARKING LOT.

So right now I am limited to walk-in business.

And in walks my first business.

I explain to the client that I charge four dollars a day, plus expenses. Possibly including some international travel, and the rental of a tugboat.

And I hand him my business card.

I ask my administrative assistant to open a new file. But I do not see him in the office. Though he has left a note.

But he is not sick. He is where he has been every day since finding out that the Home Despot sells dollar hot dogs.

His addiction to dollar hot dogs is crippling our finances.

And thus I have given him a written warning.

FAILURE, INC.
WRITTEN WARNING:
YOUR HOT DOG
ADDICTION IS
CRIPPLING OUR
FINANCES.

His response to the warning indicates a certain lack of commitment to the business.

And so I am left to create my own case files. Like for our newest case. Which I illustrate with a certain flourish.

But my illustration work is interrupted by someone more annoying than my administrative assistant.

"Well, hello, Tim. What a surprise to see you here."

It is Mr. Moskins. Father of classmate Molly Moskins. And just as annoying.

"I'm looking for a new cabinet to store all my maps," he says, cleaning his glasses with his shirt. "Mrs. Moskins says I have to put them in the garage. I guess she thinks they're taking up too much space in the house. So I need a cabinet that's nice and waterproof."

I stare at Mr. Moskins, hoping he won't stay long.

"Are you here with your mother?" he asks.

I nod.

"Very good," he says. "I haven't seen her since our Chicago trip. What section of the store is she in?"

I think fast.

"A private section," I answer. "She doesn't want to be disturbed."

"I didn't know Home Despot had private sections," he says. "Why is she in a private section?"

"I have to go now, Mr. Moskins. But if you must know, it's serious."

"Serious?" he asks.

"Yes," I answer, pausing for effect. "She's having a bad hair day."

CHAPTER 19

Larry, Merry, and No Tooth Fairy

I was never compensated by the Tooth Fairy for my missing tooth.

This despite the nice note I wrote to her.

Dear Tooth Fairy,
Please give me
money
or this could
get ugly.
—TIMMY

I suspect the lack of compensation was due to the Tooth Fairy's fear of Scary Larry and Merry Nightmare Before Christmas.

And I don't blame the Tooth Fairy for being cautious. Because things have been tense in the house ever since Timmy's Great Rebellion Against Orthodontics.

THIS

I tried to explain to my mother the necessity of dismembering Mickey Molar.

Mickey
Molar
(R.I.P.)

But she was having none of it.

Nor was she listening to the logical clues I tried to present to her about Dr. Alfredo Goni's true intentions.

Like his name tag.

Which read like this:

A.GONI

And if a name pronounced "agony" doesn't clue you in, there's nothing more I can do for you.

So the only thing I can think of is that my mother is just too distracted planning her upcoming wedding.

Which is yet another situation I am trying to advise her on.

CHAPTER 20

Ashes, Ashes, We All Fall Down

The piano lessons at Ms. Hardie-Heeron's house have gone no better than the lessons she once gave at my house.

Mostly because I am not familiar with the furnishings contained in an old woman's dusty and cluttered home. Things like odd chairs and homemade jam and too many vases.

All of which created a minor incident when Ms. Hardie-Heeron asked me to remove the gum from my mouth and I didn't have a place to put it.

So now I have to play the piano knowing that Ms. Hardie-Heeron is keeping dead guys in a jar.

And that is something that not even the Buppy Guppy is comfortable with.

I would complain about these unusual cir-cumstances to my mother, but I know she will not listen. Because ever since the shredding of Mickey Molar, she has been punishing me by insisting that I practice the piano more than ever.

And that is a problem.

Because with school in the morning and my detective work in the afternoon, I do not have the time.

So I have been getting up at 6:00 a.m. to practice.

And that has shown me a brand-new side of Merry, whose limitless love of others appears to have limits.

But I cannot stop. Because I must always listen to my mother.

And this has led to an escalation in tensions between Merry and myself.

Most of which involve high-velocity shoes.

I do not know why Merry throws shoes. But I do know that she is profoundly nearsighted. And thus, none of the shoes have connected with my precious bean.

Though one vicious stiletto did connect with Choppin' Carrots.

And the shoe hurling has caused *me* to escalate tensions as well.

Particularly when it comes to the music Merry and Larry listen to at bedtime. Which, although they use headphones, is loud enough to keep me awake in Death Valley.

I would have complained sooner. But my complaints are undermined by my administrative assistant, whose response to the loud music has been wholly inappropriate:

So on the night I finally complained, Merry and Larry were hesitant to comply. And thus I issued two friendly reminders, which were (1) this is my room and (2) they are invading Huns. And with that, Merry and Larry acceded to my demands and lowered their music.

And I slept well.

Though when I woke up, I looked different.

CHAPTER
21

Is That You, Baby, or
Just a Brilliant Detective?

I do not know which of the sisters gave me a new hairdo, mascara, painted nails, and lipstick.

And I do not care.

For the joke is on them.

Because if my close call with Mr. Moskins in Home Despot taught me anything, it was that I cannot risk my mother finding out about my new office.

Meaning that from now on I will do my office work undercover.

So deeply undercover that if Mr. Moskins were to visit again, he would have no idea who I was.

And I already have my first disguise.

My new disguise coincides with a brand-new incentive program I have begun to attract more clients.

The way a cash rebate works is this:

1. A client hires me as their detective and pays me my customary four dollars a day.

2. I then give them a portion of their payment back in cash.

That dollar I give back is called a cash incentive.

And to give my clients a further incentive, I have temporarily eliminated the four-dollar-a-day charge.

It was a brilliant marketing move.

And suddenly, business is booming.

CHAPTER
22
All in All, It's Just Another Rollo in the Hall

The shorter school days have given Toots less classroom time to eat jelly beans.

So now she is starting earlier.

As in the moment the first bell rings.

I know this for a fact because Rollo Tookus is still arriving at precisely 6:00 a.m. every day and patiently awaiting the opening of the classroom door at eight o'clock.

But the doors do not open at eight o'clock.

And when Rollo puts his ear to the class-room door, he can hear Toots in there, loudly chomping.

So class now starts twenty minutes late every day.

And it really doesn't matter.

For now there is no instruction at all.

Instead, Toots just leaves a brief notation on the classroom's whiteboard.

For those who do not know, "silent reading time" is teacher code for "I have better
things to do."

As in eat jelly beans.

And Toots's early-morning sugar frenzies
are now being followed by late-morning sugar
crashes.

Meaning that from 10:00 a.m. until the
final bell rings at noon, she does this:

This has led to a number of changes in the school curriculum.

Such as the migration of the dodgeball game from outdoors on the playground to indoors in the classroom.

So to save our precious beans, Rollo and I move into the storage cupboard.

And it is there that he gives me the worst news of my young life.

"It's true," says Rollo. "Because of the strike. They're saying that the days with the substitute teachers aren't gonna count."

"Aren't gonna count?!" I shout. "That's an insult to Toots! That woman has done her best to deliver a top-notch educational experience!"

"So what now?" I ask Rollo.

"I don't know," he says. "But it's a problem. My mom has planned this whole big European vacation for our family that was supposed to start the day school gets out. And I don't think she can cancel it."

A dodgeball slams into the side of our abode, rattling our fragile existence.

"The whole thing is a very big inconvenience," adds Rollo.

"HA!" I fire back. "You think *you're* inconvenienced? How about me? I have a detective business that can't start up again until school ends! This could be its death knell!"

"I thought you started up again anyway," says Rollo.

"I know nothing!" I reply. "And you know nothing. And even if you do know something, that something is nothing. And nothing is never something. So dwell on that, Rollo Tookus!"

"I'd rather not," says Rollo. "It doesn't make any sense."

"*You* don't make any sense," I tell Rollo. "And now you've insulted me. So good-bye. I am leaving this storage cupboard and will not be conversing with you again until you see fit to apologize."

I open the cupboard doors and am confronted by the bright light of day.

And the dim light of these two:

So I return to my sheltered abode.
And am gloriously kind.

CHAPTER
23
Jarring Developments

My reconciliation with Rollo Tookus is well timed.

Because his life is now in disarray.

For ever since the school started dismissing students at noon, it has left the library open for studying. But now, with school funds dwindling, it is closing the library at noon too.

So Rollo's history of studying history from noon to three is now history.

And today he can't study at home, either. Because his mother and father are going to something called an academic conference. And they don't want Rollo home alone. Where I suppose he could do crazy things.

Like read even more.

So Rollo's mother asked my mother if he could spend the afternoon at our apartment. And my mother, over my objection, agreed.

"You're taking a tremendous risk," I warn Rollo on the walk home. "For my life is now filled with dangerous loons."

But Rollo is too absorbed in his history book to listen.

So when we get inside my apartment, we are immediately greeted by Loon No. 1, a.k.a. Merry Nightmare Before Christmas.

And Rollo, in a bout of insanity, does this:

"What were you thinking?" I ask Rollo, pulling him back into the apartment hallway. "Do you have any idea who she is?"

"She's your cousin."

"She's my *loon* of a cousin. The one who loves babies' smiles and subway tiles and killers' style and guys named Kyle."

"Oh," says Rollo. "Well, she seemed nice."

"Dangerous loons *always* seem nice," I explain to the inexperienced Rollo. "That's what makes them dangerous."

But I am cut short by the person walking down our hall. And there is too little time to jump down the trash chute.

"You must be Rollo," says Loon No. 2, a.k.a. Scary Larry, a.k.a. Doctor Death, a.k.a. the Grim Reaper, a.k.a. the Doomsdame, a.k.a. Rollo's future killer.

"Hi," he says back.

And then, in what will become known to history as the Most Inexplicable Bit of Inexplicable Idiocy That Has Ever Occurred and Simply Cannot Be Explained by Any Sane Human Being, Rollo does the utterly unthinkable:

"You have just committed the most grievous, awful, terrible, calamitous, dreadful, shocking, atrocious, appalling act of your entire life," I announce to Rollo after Larry walks inside. "Which will not be long. For now you will die."

And Rollo, wholly unaware of the danger he is now in, responds with this:

"I think she's pretty."

I am frozen in horror, my gift of the gab silenced by the indecencies spilling forth from Rollo's mouth.

"What's the problem?" says Rollo. "I just think she has nice hair."

But I cannot respond.

Because my mother is grabbing my hand as she strides quickly out of the apartment.

"C'mon, Timmy," she says. "We're late for the orthodontist. And I have to get back to work."

"But I'm with Rollo today, remember?"

"Bring him along," she says, running for the open elevator.

So Rollo comes along.

And on the drive to the orthodontist's office, I just stare at him in the backseat as he reads.

"What's the big deal?" asks Rollo. "I just thought your cousins were nice."

"Not another word, Rollo."

We finally arrive at Dr. Agony's office, and this time there is no fake nose and no Mickey Molar.

And no Dr. Agony.

Who, exposed as the counterintelligence drill-happy agent that he is, wants no part of Timmy Failure.

And thus he has handed us off to his partner, a fellow orthodontist, who from behind a large desk gives my mother a long, boring speech, the only part of which I catch is "too young for braces."

So with great relief, I walk out of the ortho-dontist's office, knowing that I have escaped the evil clutches of Dr. Agony.

And I rejoin Rollo Tookus in the waiting room.

And am shocked at what I see.

"What a fun place!" Rollo exclaims as we walk back to the car. "They gave me stuffed animals and giant toothbrushes and coloring books!"

"Good for you," my mother says to Rollo. "Maybe one day you can come here for your own teeth."

"I sure hope so!" says Rollo.

But I am so fed up with Rollo that I do not speak to him on the drive home.

And when we arrive, my mother drops the two of us off.

"Don't forget you have your piano lesson at four o'clock!" she shouts from the car. "Rollo can stay with Larry and Merry if he doesn't want to go."

I have half a mind to *let* him stay with Merry and Larry. And *let* him get eaten by unicorns.

But I'm a detective. And we have a code.

STATE REGULATION OF DETECTIVES

Section 141(a)

Thou shall not let thy best friend be eaten by unicorns.

So I take him with me to see Ms. Hardie-Heeron.

Who, with any luck, will put Rollo in a jar.

CHAPTER
24
Wise Men Say Only Fools Hire Molly

Rollo was right.

And that is something I never thought I'd say.

Not right about Larry.

Or Merry.

Or Dr. Agony.

All of whom he grossly misjudged.

But about school. And it being extended.

Because weeks of boring half days passed, and when the last day of school came, school just kept right on going.

Into my precious summer.

And if there were ever any doubt about the legality of continuing my detective business, it was gone now.

Because the last day of school that my mother and I had agreed upon had come and gone.

And it wasn't my fault school decided to add more.

But what is doubly tragic about the extended school year is that I could have used the summer break to deal with my exploding caseload.

Which has now grown so large that I have had to hire another assistant.

The drawbacks of hiring Molly Moskins are many:

1. She is a nuisance.
2. She smiles too much.
3. She smells like a tangerine.

TANGERINE

But there are also advantages. The main one being that she is barred from spending time with me (read my last book for details).

Thus, she would be the *last* person to tell anyone that she and I are doing detective work. And even though I view my current work as permissible, my mother would not.

Because she is a mother.

And has only one answer to everything.

Thus, we cannot risk being spotted doing detective work. So I have insisted that she, like me, wear a disguise.

And thus, we are the King of Rock and Roll.

I do not know who the King of Rock and Roll is. But Molly does. And so now I am King No. 1 and she is King No. 2.

I would talk more about King No. 3, but he is so busy eating dollar hot dogs that he is the reason I had to hire King No. 2 in the first place.

And frankly, he is now so fat that I do not think he could work if he wanted to.

And that is unfortunate. Because with my incentive program in place, I now have an endless stream of clients.

And so my reputation is growing fast. Which means that soon I will attract bigger cases.

Like tracking down forgers.

And kidnappers.

And killers.

Which means that soon I will have my towering office in the sky.

Though perhaps not without negotiation.

CHAPTER
25

Oh, Say Can You See Rollo by the Dawn's Early Light

Merry and Larry are getting on a ferry.

To some summer retreat on an island where they learn something.

I do not know what.

Though I can guess.

My mother has to get them to the dock at 6:30 a.m. And she does not want to leave me at home alone.

So I can either go with her to take Larry and Merry to the ferry or go to school two hours early.

And for the first time in my young life, I choose school.

And my mother isn't worried about my going to school early. Because she knows that Rollo will be there.

Which is good.

Because I need the extra time to criticize him.

For his shaking of hands with Merry.

And his hugging of Scary Larry.

And his taking of all he could carry.

And I didn't even tell you about the travesty that was my piano lesson.

Where Rollo Tookus, betrayer of his best friend, volunteered to play the complete works of Choppin' Carrots.

All of which thrilled Ms. Hardie-Heeron so much that she stuck a giant gold star on his sweatshirt.

But I will try not to be *too* hard on Rollo, because I know that he feels the teachers' strike has derailed his academic future and that soon he will be cleaning people's windshields at stoplights.

And I also know that Rollo has some good traits.

For in a world filled with teachers who abandon us and mothers who marry the doorman, he is at least consistent. His 6:00 a.m. arrival at our classroom door, Room No. 6, is as dependable as the dawn.

Which on this morning crests above the

horizon beyond the playground asphalt.

Filling the dark halls of school with soft gray light.

Revealing rows of school lockers.

And lines of lunch tables.

And Room No. 6.

With no Rollo.

CHAPTER 26
For Your Mismatched Eyes Only

It is in the pressure cooker of life's tragedies that one learns the true nature of a detective.

And Rollo's untimely demise is one of those moments.

So while most would panic, I do not.

For I am focused.

And my detective mind is racing like a Thoroughbred on ice skates.

And my first priority is to discreetly get word to my associate Molly Moskins. The opportunity for which arises during silent reading time, when she passes me a note.

Which says this:

So I write her a note back:

Her reaction is silence. So I write her a follow-up note:

This breaks her out of her stupor. And she quickly scribbles a note back:

CHAPTER
27
Boy, Interrupted

When the noon bell rings, I race to my detective office, besieged by impertinent questions.

And when I arrive at my office, I am greeted by another unwelcome surprise.

An official-looking notice taped to the door.

So I yank it down and read it.

ALL GARDEN
SHEDS MUST GO

ALL SHEDS
— HALF OFF —
INVENTORY TO BE
ELIMINATED!

And I know immediately what it means.

That at the moment of the most important investigation of my life, Home Despot is going to take away my office.

And that is fatal, because a detective office is the only place a detective can think in safety and in peace.

Which means that I have very little time left to solve the mystery of the disappearing Rollo.

And more interruptions than ever.

CHAPTER
28
Lord of the Ring Bearers

My world collapsing, my mother piles it on.

"You're going to be the ring bearer at the wedding," she says over dinner.

"What the heck's a ring bearer?" I inquire.

"You walk down the aisle with the ring."

"You mean I just walk the thing from one end of the aisle to the other?"

"Well, yes," she answers. "In a manner of speaking."

"And then what? Do I throw it into a volcano like Frodo?"

"No, you don't throw it into a volcano. You just walk it down the aisle."

"Well, if all you need is to move the thing from one place to another, can't you just call FedEx or somebody?"

"No," she says. "FedEx will not be my ring bearer. You will. And Merry and Larry will be bridesmaids."

And at the mere mention of their names,

I want to inform my mother that the evil sisters are two of the suspects in Rollo's disappearance. Which is why they've both fled to their island "retreat."

But I say nothing.

Because there's another suspect I have to investigate first.

CHAPTER
29
Molly Impossible

"You're to roam around the house unseen and unheard," I inform my associate. "Looking for clues. Gathering evidence. Remember, this person may be responsible for Rollo's disappearance. Now are you ready?"

"I think so," says Molly Moskins.

So I ring the doorbell.

And when the door opens, we are confronted by our shifty suspect.

"You're early," says Ms. Hardie-Heeron.

"I am," I answer. "Because I brought along a valued associate. An associate who's thinking of taking lessons from you."

"Greetings!" says Molly.

Ms. Hardie-Heeron looks down at her watch and back up at us.

"Fine," she says. "But give me a minute. I have to turn off the stove. I was cooking my dinner for tonight."

We walk into Ms. Hardie-Heeron's

mothball-scented living room, now vaguely accented by the stench of boiling fish.

And Molly, unable to let our secret plan unfold naturally, blurts out this:

"I HAVE TO GO TO THE BATHROOM!"

"What?" says Ms. Hardie-Heeron, wandering out of her kitchen with a wooden spoon.

"I have to go to the bathroom," Molly says again. "But don't worry. I won't snoop through your personal belongings or steal valuables."

Ms. Hardie-Heeron stares silently at Molly. As do I.

"Second door on the left," says my piano teacher.

Molly skips down the hall and I sit next to Ms. Hardie-Heeron on the piano bench.

"Turn to the third song in your Buppy Guppy songbook," she says to me. "And see if you can play that one all the way through."

So I leaf through the book to that page.

And see that the song title is uncomfortably appropriate.

The Buppy Guppy Sneaks Through the House of the Puppy

Suddenly, I begin to think that my piano teacher is on to us. Has perhaps been tipped off by informants.

And I contemplate yelling out our prearranged code word that subtly indicates we are abandoning the operation.

But I don't have the chance.

Because I hear the sound of footsteps in the kitchen.

And I know instantly what is happening.

For in prepping Molly Moskins for the delicate mission, I had made it clear that Ms. Hardie-Heeron had put her husband in a jar.

And from that, I know that Molly is thinking that Ms. Hardie-Heeron put *Rollo* in a jar.

Which tells me that Molly is going to search through the kitchen, where she will eventually stumble upon Ms. Hardie-Heeron's large collection of homemade jams.

And it is here that I need to tell you something else.

Which is this:

Not fully trusting Molly to complete the mission, I enlisted the help of my equally untrustworthy administrative assistant, thinking that two half-trustworthy associates add up to one trusty one.

So while Molly and I were welcomed through the front door, my administrative assistant snuck in through the back door.

The one that leads through the kitchen pantry.

And it is at this point, while I am playing "The Buppy Guppy Sneaks Through the House of the Puppy," that my large detective brain detects a flaw in the plan.

And that is that my overweight administrative assistant is going to spot Ms. Hardie-Heeron's homemade jam. And once he does, he is going to break off the lids and lick every one of those jars clean.

And Molly Moskins, who is now in the kitchen, is going to witness that and think only one thing:

And her screams will scare my bear.

And my bear will fall.

And the pantry will look like this:

And if all that unfolds and my piano teacher sees it, I will be in a situation that not even the great Timmy Failure can explain away.

Not to Ms. Hardie-Heeron.

And certainly not to my mother.

And so, when I hear the continued sound of Molly's footsteps in the kitchen, I try to mask them by playing "The Buppy Guppy" with extra gusto.

But it doesn't work. Because I can still hear Molly.

And so can my piano teacher.

So when she rises to investigate the source of the noise, I yell out a code word that is slightly less coded than the others.

Which Molly does.

And as she bolts for the back door, she runs past the pot on Ms. Hardie-Heeron's stove. Where she sees this:

Which she assumes is Rollo Tookus.

And so my associate runs screaming out the back door.

And my piano teacher follows.

And the King of Rock and Roll eats Rollo.

CHAPTER
30
Failure. Tim Failure.

"It wasn't Rollo in the pot," I explain to Molly Moskins over the phone. "And he wasn't in any jam jar, either."

But she's too shaken up to listen.

SHAKEN-
UP
MOLLY

So I give her the day off.

So she can do what she always does when she is shaken up.

Which is to eat too much ice cream.

And it is a day I need as well.

Because I'm being fitted for a tuxedo.

"Just wait till everyone at the wedding sees you!" my mother says when I walk out of the changing room. "You look like an international spy! Like James Bond!"

"I do look rather refined," I answer.

She smiles.

"Just know that this in no way changes my attitude toward the wedding," I remind her. "For which I still vote two thumbs down. Way down."

TWO THUMBS DOWN. WAY DOWN.

"I know, Timmy. You've told me. Now go put your normal clothes back on."

"I can't wear this home?"

"No, you can't wear it home, silly," she says. "You'll wrinkle it. And it needs to look perfect for the wedding."

So I listen to my mother.

And do not wear it home.

But I do wear it somewhere else.

CHAPTER 31

Angel of the Silence

"Where were you on the morning of Rollo Tookus's disappearance?" I ask Angel de Manzanas Naranjas in one of the library's private study rooms, which I'm using as an interrogation chamber.

"Is Rollo gone?" responds Angel.

"Don't play dumb with me, Manzanas Naranjas. Because this room can get real rough real fast, if you know what I mean."

"Right," says Angel, putting his feet on the table.

"And where's your partner-in-dodgeball-crime?" I ask, turning up the heat. "That little rat Scutaro."

"Bathroom," says Angel.

"Oh, really?" I ask. "And why is that?"

"Because he needed to go to the bathroom."

The door to the room swings open. And in peers Nunzio Benedici.

"Hey, Angel, you seen Scutaro?"

"Bathroom," says Angel.

"Can't you see I'm busy?" I ask Nunzio.

"Sorry," he answers. "I wanted Scutaro to sign my yearbook."

And it's true.

It's yearbook day.

The day late in the semester when we all get our annual school yearbook.

And I do not like it. Because it's filled with stupid things like photos of the debating team (I don't debate), and the cheerleading squad (I don't cheerlead), and the school band (I don't band).

In fact, the yearbook covers every single sport, hobby, club, and social organization in the entire school.

Except for the one that held the most promise.

The one that I formed.

And thus I am against the yearbook.

And I am especially against the ritual whereby each of the students asks the other students to sign their yearbook and write some frivolous banality.

For this reason, I try to make the things I write in yearbooks both meaningful and instructive.

WHEN BEING ATTACKED BY A PUMA, BE NOISY AND MAKE YOURSELF LARGE. — Timmy

Thus, I am besieged by requests to sign other people's yearbooks. And knowing this, I put a sign on the outside of the interrogation room door.

INTERROGATION IN PROGRESS (I will sign your yearbook later.) —T. Failure

"So where were we?" I ask Angel when I return to the room.

"You were telling me why you're wearing that stupid suit."

"Ah, yes," I say, ignoring the subject's taunt. "You were telling me how you and the ratlike Scutaro pelted Rollo with deadly dodgeballs."

Angel just stares at me.

For he is dumbfounded by my brilliant question. A question that assumes a fact the suspect has not yet revealed. Thereby tricking the suspect into now admitting something he has not yet admitted.

A classic interrogation technique.

"Not in here," answers Angel.

"What?" I ask, now confused myself.

It is then that I see he is not talking to me, but to someone he sees through the interrogation room window.

"Scutaro's not in here?" asks Toody Tululu, barging in.

"Bathroom," says Angel.

"Oh," says Toody, "I wanted him to—"

"Sign your stupid yearbook!" I interrupt. "We *know*. You want Scutaro to sign it! You want me to sign it! Didn't you see what I wrote on the door?"

"Yeah, but I don't want you to sign it," says Toody.

"Of course you don't want me to sign it *right now*," I answer. "Out of respect for the fact that I am conducting an interrogation."

She stares at the suspect. "Will *you* sign my yearbook, Angel?"

"No, he won't sign your yearbook!" I bark. "He's busy, too!"

Angel takes her yearbook and signs it.

And it is as dull as it is uneducated.

He hands the yearbook back to Toody.

Toody leaves.

"You spelled 'rule' wrong," I tell him.

"Don't care," he says.

"Fine," I say, conceding his educational deficiencies. "Now tell me what you and Scutaro did to Rollo."

"You're boring me," he answers. "Go talk to Scutaro. He's in the bathroom."

So I slam my fist down on the table.

"Okay, Manzanas Naranjas, I was hoping I wouldn't have to go this route. Wouldn't have to get tough. But you leave me little choice."

And faster than I can say "uncooperative suspect," Angel lunges across the table and rips my shirt in two.

And as I look down at the torn wedding clothes I'm not supposed to be wearing, the door opens.

"You're late for dodgeball," says Scutaro.

"Coming," answers Angel.

And as he brushes past me, he yanks my sign off the door.

And scribbling something on the other side, he hands it back to me.

CHAPTER 32

If the Bear Don't Fit, You Must All Quit

The Rollo investigation has caused me to put off all my other cases.

And thus, my Mr. Froggie phone is bursting with unplayed messages.

YOU HAVE 54
—RRRIBBITT—
MESSAGES.

But I only have so much time before my covert garden shed headquarters is taken away. And with nowhere else to work, that could mean the end of the biggest investigation of my life.

So with the clock ticking, I call an emergency meeting at our headquarters to go over the status of the investigation and update the suspect list.

But someone is too fat to fit through the office door.

And so the meeting is canceled.

CHAPTER
33
Down in the Pits

And the meeting is not the only thing that is canceled.

For so are my piano lessons.

Which was kindly explained to my mother this way:

When what she really wanted to say was this:

And the cancellation of the piano lessons is welcome news.

Because Molly and I are in a race against time to find out what happened to Rollo. And apprehend the vicious culprits.

And so when Merry and Larry return from their "retreat," they fall right into our clutches. And we grill Larry first.

But because of her headphones, she does not hear me. So I gently repeat the inquiry.

"Hi," says Larry, glancing at my associate. "I don't think I know you."

"I'm Molly. And you have pretty hair."

I elbow my colleague in the ribs.

"And we'd like to ask you some questions," Molly adds, frowning at me.

"Okay," answers Larry. "Let me turn down my music."

She turns down the music.

"Okay," she says. "What do you need?"

And I drop the bombshell.

"For you to be attached to our lie-detector machine."

Now I should say here that I no longer have my original lie-detector machine, which was this:

The way it worked was that if you pulled the string and the cow mooed, you were scientifically proven to be a liar.

But then the string broke. And the dial got stuck on the duck. And the whole thing became rather distracting during tense, high-level interrogations.

So now we have the next best thing:
The Mollygraph.

"One end of these wires will be attached to your forehead," I explain to Larry. "And the other end will be attached to my associate."

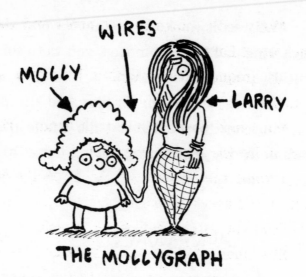

THE MOLLYGRAPH

"It works because I have a sixth sense for when people are lying," adds Molly. "But you're pretty. So I don't think you'd lie."

I elbow Molly in the ribs again. She stomps on my foot.

Larry laughs.

"Sure," says Larry. "Go for it."

So Molly attaches the wires and asks the first question.

"How do you get your hair so pretty?"

"Stop!" I interrupt. "Yes or no questions only! And not about hair!"

Molly looks down at her notes and then back up at Larry.

"Is frequent conditioning how you get your hair so pretty?"

"Oh, good gosh!" I interrupt again. "That does it. Let *me* ask the questions."

I yank the notes away from Molly and stare into Larry's lone eye.

"Did you kill Rollo Tookus?" I ask.

She laughs. "Who's Rollo Tookus?"

"Yes or no answers only," I remind her.

"But I don't know who he is."

"Fine," I say. "Have you ever killed *anybody*?"

"Hmm," she answers. "I guess I've killed flies. And maybe some ants."

"No, no, no," I groan. "Have you ever killed a *human-type person*?"

"Oh," she replies. "No."

I follow the length of the wires down to Molly's head.

"PLLLLLBBBTHHHHHH," says Molly.

"What was that?" I ask her.

"It's a raspberry. It's the sound I'm gonna make when somebody tells the truth."

"Can't you make a better sound than that?"

"Okay," she answers. "DOO doo do do do do DO doo dooo do."

"What's that?"

"Circus music."

"That's not any better!"

"Well, what if I just make fart sounds with my armpit?"

"Arrgghh!" I cry. "Then just go back to the stupid raspberry."

"PLLLLLBBBTHHHHHH," says Molly.

"WAIT TILL I ASK LARRY A QUESTION!"

But I can't ask Larry a question.

Because now she is texting someone.

"Can't that wait?" I ask, my frustration growing. "We are in the middle of a *felony investigation*."

"Sorry," answers Larry. "But it can't wait. My friend is buying shoes. And she wants to know what kind to buy."

"PLLLLLBBBTHHHHHH," says Molly. "She's telling the truth."

"That wasn't one of my questions!" I remind my associate.

But she is not listening.

For she is peering over Larry's shoulder at the shoe photos being texted to her.

"Oooooh, that one's really pretty," says Molly.

"Isn't it?" answers Larry.

"I would totally get those shoes," adds my associate.

"Did you or did you not kill Rollo Tookus?" I ask, breaking up the shoe party.

Larry looks up at me and then back down to her phone.

"Yes," replies Larry.

"Yes, you killed him?" I ask, surprised by the casual admission.

"Yes, my friend should buy these shoes."

"PLLLLLBBBTHHHHHH," says Molly. "They're good shoes."

"STOP DOING THAT!" I shout at Molly, yanking the wires off her and Larry and stomping out of the bedroom. "You are both making a mockery of the criminal justice system!"

But as I walk out of the room, Larry follows.

"Hey," she says to me in the bedroom hallway. "I don't know what you're playing, but I didn't mean to frustrate you."

"I'm not *playing*," I answer. "You're a suspect in an investigation."

"Okay, well, whatever you're doing, I didn't mean to ignore you. I just like shoes. And that's the truth."

And with that, Molly steps out into the hallway.

To add one more thing.

PHHT
PHHT
PHHT

CHAPTER 34

The Shoe Fits

It is early morning.

And as I get ready for school, my mother hands me her phone.

"Be nice," she says.

"Hello, Mr. Failure," says Doorman Dave. "I won't keep you long. I know you're on your way to school."

"I am. And my devotion to school leaves me little time for idle chitchat."

"Well, just give me a minute," he says.

So I sit on the piano bench under the watchful gaze of Choppin' Carrots.

"What do you want?" I ask.

"Listen. I know you're under a lot of pressure, and I know you're not thrilled with all the wedding stuff, but if you could, go easy on your mom about the whole thing. She's got enough stress, what with trying to figure out catering and guest lists and all that junk."

"Uh, for your information, Doorman Dave—"

"Just Dave."

"For your information, Dave, the school year has been extended. And with you two lovebirds being so shortsighted as to set the wedding on a *Friday*, there is now a good chance I won't be there. Because school comes first, you know. Academics are very important to me."

And as I say it, I don't like the look I get from Choppin' Carrots.

So I poke him in the eye.

"Right," says Dave. "Well, when we originally set the wedding date, it was not on a school day. It was summer. But I'm sure that will all sort itself out. And you're not gonna miss our wedding."

"Don't tell me what to do, Dave."

"Timmy . . ."

I stand on the piano bench and shout.

"DON'T TELL ME WHAT TO DO, DAVE!"

And as I say it, I am proud.

Unbowed.

And perhaps too loud.

CHAPTER
35
The Unusual Suspects

"So it was either her or her or her," I say, pointing at the pictures of Ms. Hardie-Heeron, Merry, and Larry on our garden shed wall.

We are having a closed-door meeting of Failure, Inc., before school because (1) I no longer have to practice the piano and (2) we need to maximize our dwindling time at the garden shed.

"Right," says Molly Moskins, examining the pictures. "Because Rollo was exposed to all of them on the day he came to your house."

"Exactly," I say.

"But wasn't he exposed to your orthodontist too?"

"Yes," I answer. "But he's not a suspect."

"Why not?"

"Because orthodontists only torture. They don't kill."

There is a knock on the garden shed door. And an outstretched hand.

"I'm not giving you any more money," I tell my administrative assistant. "Look at you."

My bear looks down at his belly and back up at me. And promises no more hot dogs.

"Fine," I tell him. "I'll give you a dollar,

but you have to spend it on healthy food."

He takes the dollar from my hand and stomps off.

"*Healthy* food," I repeat after him.

"Who were you giving money to?" asks Molly as I return to the meeting.

"No one," I say. "Now go on with the list of suspects."

"There aren't any more," she says. "Except maybe Angel and Scutaro."

"It's not them," I answer. "Too dumb. "Could you imagine a ransom note written by Angel?"

"Well, they do like to pummel Rollo with dodgeballs," says Molly. "And that can scramble the old bean." She points to her head.

"Right," I say. "But that vicious game of dodgeball wasn't their idea."

"Then whose idea was it?"

I stare into Molly's mismatched pupils. "Meet me at school in half an hour."

CHAPTER 36

A Hole in His Story

My plan in motion, I race to school on the Bra-Mobile.

Where I am stunned by a sight in the donut shop.

CHAPTER
37
The Sweet Smell
of Failure

With some suspects you must use espionage.

With others you must intimidate.

And with some you must bribe.

"Donuts?" says Toots. "How did you know I love donuts?"

She grabs one out of the box and shoves it in her mouth.

"Buh why aw yu givin' thmm tuh me?" she mumbles, her crammed mouth spitting out donut crumbs.

"For information," I answer.

She swallows the donut. "What kind of information?"

And so I deliver the hammer.

"Admitting that you caused the disappearance of Rollo Tookus."

Toots stares at the donuts. Her eyes widen.

"Okay," she says. "I admit it."

"I knew it!" I cry. "Your sugar addiction and aggressive dodgeball tactics were a not-so-subtle indicator of your nefarious ways."

Until I see a second box of donuts slide across the table and come to rest in front of Toots.

"What are those?" asks Toots.

"Maple bars," answers Molly, who apparently missed the part of the plan where we said *I* would be bribing the suspect.

"Maple bars!" drools Toots. "Those are my favorite! But why are *you* giving me donuts?"

"Information," says Molly Moskins before I can stop her.

"What kind of information?"

"Did you or did you not have anything to do with the disappearance of Rollo Tookus?"

The suspect's eyes dart between me and the second box of donuts.

"Well, what do you *want* me to say?" asks Toots.

"That you did not," says Molly slowly and deliberately. "Because I *love* my teachers. And I'd hate to think you could be anything but fantastical."

"Then I most definitely did not!" exclaims Toots.

"Yaaaaaaay!" cheers Molly. "Then enjoy your maple bar donuts!"

And with that, the suspect clutches both boxes to her chest and waddles off as fast as her high trousers will take her.

And I turn to my associate.

CHAPTER 38

Bridesmaid of Frankenstein

We have one suspect left to confront.

And she is hogging the bathroom.

"Remember, this is called good cop/bad cop," I tell Molly. "And if she ever comes out of there, we're gonna use it on her."

"Tell me what it is again," she says.

"We've been over this ten times. *You* act reasonable. *I* act unreasonable."

"And you're sure it works?"

"Of course I'm sure. The suspect wants to talk to you, because you're kind. Otherwise, they have to deal with rough and tough me."

"Rough and tough you," repeats Molly. "I like that."

"But remember," I remind her, "this suspect is a frowny-faced dangerous loon."

And as I say it, the bathroom door opens.

And out walks the frowny-faced dangerous loon.

"Who are you?" I ask. "And what did you do with Merry?"

"I am Merry," she says. "And I'm trying on my dress for the wedding. Your mother asked me to be a bridesmaid."

I peer into the laundry hamper to look for the real Merry.

"That's the most beautiful dress I've ever seen in my whole life," says Molly.

"Well, thank you," answers Merry. "Are you one of Timmy's friends?"

"I am. I'm Molly Moskins."

"Well, it's nice to meet you, Molly Moskins," she says, then turns to me. "And Timmy, your mother told me to tell you that she's not going to be able to do the Take Your

Child to Work thing. She's too busy."

"What's a Take Your Child to Work thing?" I reply.

"Toots told us about it, Timmy," says Molly. "When she woke up from her nap. We're gonna have a special day where we each follow one of our parents to work."

"That's ridiculous," I say. "I have a business to run."

"A business to run?" asks Merry, combing her hair. "I hope you don't mean your detective business. Because your mother told me all about it."

"I know nothing!" I declare.

"I think you do know something," says Merry, admiring her dress in the mirror. "Like the fact that you're not allowed to *do* any detective work right now. Because you're supposed to be concentrating on school."

She turns to look at me.

"You're not doing detective work right now, are you, Timmy? Because I'd hate to have to tell your mother."

"Spy! Traitor! Shoe thrower!" I shout.

"Does this mean the interrogation is canceled?" asks Molly.

"What interrogation?" asks Merry.

"NO interrogation!" I yell.

Panicked, the good cop hugs Merry's leg.

"I LOVE YOU!" cries Molly.

"What are you doing?" asks Merry.

"Being the good cop," answers Molly. "And I love you very much. Even if you *are* an evil criminal."

"Well, aren't you sweet," says Merry, lifting Molly up into her arms. "I love you too, Molly Moskins."

"It's a trick!" I shout.

"I was just about to do my nails," Merry says to Molly. "Would you like to help?"

"I would *love* to help," answers Molly. "I only have a brother. So I *never* get to do stuff like that."

"Well, good. Maybe I can do your nails, too."

"Run!" I cry. "You're doomed!"

But Molly presses her cheek into Merry's neck. And Merry holds her tighter.

"I *love* being good cop!" Molly confides to Merry as the two retreat down the hall. "And you're the most beautiful, wonderful person in the world!"

And the two leave.

The good cop now doomed.

The bad cop marooned.

And the bridesmaid a loon.

CHAPTER 39

In the Shadow of Greatness

Shadow Holmes is the father of Scutaro Holmes. He makes toilet plungers.

← These things

He is just as short as his son, but eleven times his circumference.

And because my mother is too busy to attend to the needs of her lone child, I am shadowing Shadow—and not her—on Take Your Child to Work Day.

Which means that I follow Shadow throughout the course of his day's activities. To conferences. To corner offices. To cafeterias. To coffee breaks.

And today is not just any day at Holmes's Toilet Supplies.

For today is Aloha Toilet Day, when

everyone dresses up in Hawaiian shirts and attends an end-of-the-workday luau, during which they pull a roasted pig out of the ground.

Presumably with a plunger.

SPLORT

All of which is considerably better than spending the day with my mother at *her* place of work.

Which is a law firm.

Where their idea of a good time is this:

About my only complaint regarding Take Your Child to Work Day is that I am not the only child present.

For I am joined by the ratlike Scutaro, whom I must remember not to call "ratlike" during the time I am with his father.

I call Scutaro "ratlike" because he is an underhanded cheater with a profound propensity to tell on other people.

Which is of little concern to me now.

Because I know something that nobody else at Holmes's Toilet Supplies knows. And it's not about plungers.

But about Rollo Tookus.

For with the suspect interrogations complete, I need just one more Failure, Inc., meeting with my associate Molly Moskins to put all the clues together and solve the biggest case of my career.

A case that will generate headlines around the globe.

Meaning that soon I will have my towering office in the sky.

Which I can see now as clearly as if it were right in front of me.

And so, when Shadow leaves me in his corner office to take Scutaro to the men's room, I close the door and put on my fashionable Hawaiian sunglasses.

And press the red button marked INTERCOM on his telephone.

"Aloha, employees of Failure, Inc.," I announce, my voice echoing throughout the many corridors of the building. "This is your founder, president, and CEO."

And as I say it, I see some of the employees stop and stare at me through the large glass wall.

And see the ratlike Scutaro, freshly back from the bathroom.

WHAT DO YOU THINK YOU'RE DOING?

And see the balloon-like Shadow, ready to burst.

And see that there is only one honorable way out.

CHAPTER 40

Crane Games

There is a large crane over my head.

"What do you think you're doing?" I yell at the Home Despot crane operator.

"Moving the sheds, kid. Back to the distribution center."

"Can't that wait?!" I ask.

"Yep," he answers, cutting the crane's engine. "'Cos it's my break. But when I come back in five minutes, they're all going on the truck."

"What was all that about?" asks Molly when I step back into the office.

"They're taking our headquarters," I answer. "We don't have much time."

"What do we do?" she asks.

"We *let me think*."

I pace the office, the suspects' pictures lining the wall.

And then, in a flash of brilliant magnificent genius, I reveal all.

"Corrina Corrina never retired!" I proclaim from atop my desk.

"From what?"

"The detective business. It was a *ruse*. A *sham*. A *charade*. All designed to make me lower my guard."

"Why would she do that?" asks Molly.

"Because she knows I'm about to dominate the entire detective world. And she wants me stopped."

"But what does that have to do with Rollo?"

"She took him hostage," I explain. "And

when she sees I'm at the top of the detective world, she's going to reveal that she has him and use him to negotiate."

As I say it, I hear the crane engine roar back to life.

"Negotiate for what, Timmy? And hurry up. We don't have much time."

"She wants my tower in the sky! My employees! My untarnished business name! Isn't it obvious?"

"It is!" answers Molly.

I look through the window and see the crane lift a garden shed at the far end of our row.

"So how did she do it?" asks Molly. *"How did she do it?"*

"Elementary," I answer. "She got the sisters into my house. They were spies. Not cousins."

"But didn't your mom say they were your cousins?"

"Of course she did! Because she wants the detective business stopped too!"

"Of course!" says Molly. "Mothers are always in on it! But what were the sisters there to do?"

"To watch me. Day and night. And feed information through their 'headphones' to Corrina Corrina. What time I go to bed. How I comb my hair. Whether I like raisins."

"Yes!" says Molly, before pausing. "But why would they watch you?"

"So Corrina Corrina could determine where I'm vulnerable. Figure out her devious point of attack."

"But your cousins *seemed so nice*," Molly wails, head in hands.

"There, there," I say, patting my associate on the back. "Life is cruel that way."

"So then what?" asks Molly.

There is a loud creak as the crane lifts another garden shed.

"So the cousins figured out that Rollo was my best friend. And decided that he would be the point of attack."

"A pawn in their vicious game!" cries Molly.

"Yes," I answer. "And that's where the piano teacher came in."

"The jar lady?"

"The jar lady," I answer. "On the day Rollo came to my house, the sisters made sure he didn't stay with them. Because they wanted him to go with me. To my piano lesson."

"Why?"

"So Hardie-Heeron could get a look at him. See if he would fit in one of her jars."

"Did he?"

"No," I answer. "Too big. Too round."

"So what then?"

"So they scrambled. Changed course. Decided on a new way to capture Rollo."

As I say it, I hear the sounds of another shed being lifted into the air. But as it rises, I hear the loud creak of wood being strained to its breaking point.

And so I look out the window.

And see my administrative assistant fall out of the double doors.

Followed by dozens of hot dogs.

"You are never working for me again!" I shout from the window to my administrative assistant. Who then gathers up as many hot dogs as he can and flees.

"What then, Timmy?" asks Molly. "What did Corrina Corrina and the sisters do next?"

"They got desperate," I answer. "And called in the big guns. The orthodontist."

"Dr. Agony?" she asks.

"Yes," I answer.

"But didn't Rollo go to the orthodontist *before* he went to Ms. Hardie-Heeron's house?"

"How am I supposed to be a genius with you always interrupting?" I cry.

"You're right! You're right!" answers Molly. "Hurry!"

"So Corrina Corrina and the sisters approached Dr. Agony. And asked him to do what orthodontists do best. Which is extract information."

"Through the use of tiny little metal bands!" shouts Molly. "On every tooth!"

"Yes!" I answer, proud of my associate's intellectual growth.

And as I answer, I hear the crane coming closer.

"Finish, Timmy, finish. What did Dr. Agony do?"

"He was stuck. Because he couldn't use his normal tactics on Rollo."

"Why not?" asks Molly.

"Because Rollo Tookus doesn't need braces."

"His teeth are perfect!" Molly adds. "So what did Dr. Agony and his evil band of orthodontists do instead?"

"They bribed the poor kid with all the Mickey Molars and giant toothbrushes he could carry."

THIS AGAIN

"And did it work?"

"You bet it worked," I answer.

"And what did they find out?" asks Molly.

I hear another garden shed rise into the sky and turn back to stare into Molly Moskins's mismatched pupils.

"That Rollo Tookus arrived at school every day at exactly 6:00 a.m."

"Of course!" answers Molly, her rapid-fire lips firing furiously. "And then Toots lured him into the classroom with a box of donuts, and Angel and Scutaro pummeled him with dodgeballs until he agreed to be taken prisoner by Corrina Corrina!"

"Slow down, slow down," I caution Molly. "You're close, but that's not exactly it. You really need to let *me* do the explaining."

"Then hurry!" Molly shouts.

And as she shouts, I hear the trudge of heavy work boots approach the garden shed.

"Okay, kids, playtime is over," says the crane operator, peering into our window. "We need to move this one."

"One minute!" says Molly. "We just need one minute."

"Fine. Just one minute," snarls the crane operator as he stomps back to his crane. "And then you're *outta here.*"

Molly turns back to face me.

"So is that it?" asks Molly. "Is everything you just explained the solution to the case? That it was *everyone* who did it? Corrina Corrina and Merry and Larry and your mother and the piano teacher and Dr. Agony and Toots and Angel and Scutaro?"

"It was a conspiracy of buffoons!" I declare, hopping back onto my desk. "We shall arrest them all for the disappearance of the round-headed Rollo Tookus."

"Hooray!" cheers Molly, before pausing. "But is that allowed? To just say everyone did it? I mean, I know I'm not a professional detective or anything, but I'm pretty sure none of the detective stories I've ever read end like that."

It is a fair point, despite being uttered by an amateur.

So I rifle through the detective code for the answer.

> **STATE REGULATION OF DETECTIVES**
>
> ## Section 11(a)
>
> **She's right. Detective stories can't end like that.**

So I check the code again for what to do when you have this many suspects.

> **STATE REGULATION OF DETECTIVES**
>
> ## Section 2342(h) – What to Do When You Have This Many Suspects:
>
> **Pick name from hat.**

And so with the crane bearing down on us, Molly and I scramble to write down every suspect's name on tiny scraps of paper that we throw into my detective hat.[2]

And as our final seconds in the shed tick away, I close my eyes and pull a piece of paper from the hat.

"Oh, my God," I say, staring at the tiny scrap. "The killer was—"

But before I can say it, a head pokes through our garden shed window.

---

2. A hat I have carried with me since *Timmy Failure 1: Mistakes Were Made.* You'll have to read it for yourself.

And it is not the crane operator.

CHAPTER
41

Rehearsal of Misfortune

Merry claims she was able to find me in a Home Despot garden shed because she saw me dipping in and out of them on our fateful trip together to find a sprinkler head.

But I know better.

Because I know that Merry is a professional spy.

And that she could find the hardiest hamster in a hamlet heaving with hamsters.

But today it was not a hamster she was trying to find.

It was a ring bearer.

For this:

THE WEDDING REHEARSAL STARTED FIFTEEN MINUTES AGO.

I THINK I CAN HOLD A RING WITHOUT PRACTICING.

Meaning that Merry's discovery of me did not just come on the eve of my solving the biggest case of a lifetime.

It also came on the day before my mother's midsummer wedding.

Which, with any luck, would not involve a certain genius detective.

CHAPTER
42

Luck Be a Lady Who Hates Me Very Much

I had an ironclad excuse for getting out of the wedding.

And that was the teachers' strike.

For it caused the school year to stretch well into the summer.

And with the wedding taking place on a Friday, that meant this:

ARE YOU COMING?

SORRY. SCHOOL DAY.

But on the one day of my life I was actually *wishing* for school, school did what it does best, and dashed my hopes, this time upon the cold stage of the school auditorium, where the striking teachers shook hands with the school district's new superintendent, thus settling the long strike.

Apparently, the old superintendent, Mr. Dobbs, was an unyielding negotiator throughout the course of the strike.

And so the school district brought in a new superintendent, one with thirty years of experience in school administration.

And even more in jelly bean consumption.

And Toots's first act as superintendent was to declare the school year officially over.

LET'S ALL GO EAT DONUTS!

Which destroyed my ironclad excuse.

And on the day of the wedding, put me in the one place I didn't want to be.

Standing next to the one doorman I didn't want to see.

And so, with my detective life destroyed and my scholarly future in shambles, I find myself clinging to just one frayed hope.

Merry.

Because Merry is an international spy.

And spies have a flair for the dramatic.

And so, when my mother is on the precipice of marital doom, Merry will no doubt spill the jelly beans.

And with any luck, that will derail the whole wedding.

And we will all go home and celebrate.

And even if *that* doesn't happen, one other thing most certainly will.

And that is that I will be grounded for the remaining seventy years of my otherwise glorious life. Beginning that very moment.

And thus I will be spared the awful spectacle of a wedding.

For which I am now standing just outside the church doors.

In a ripped shirt.

Handing to each of the arriving guests a photo of my mother and Doorman Dave.

Complete with nauseating inscription.

Come be a witness to our eternal love....

For which I feel compelled to add a caveat.

And placing the offensive card into the outstretched hands of faceless strangers, I await the arrival at the church of my mother and her bridesmaids.

Wherein Merry will tell all.

And the Mom hammer will fall.

And my detective life, now stalled . . .

will finally hit a wall.

And instead I meet a zombie.

CHAPTER 43

Dead Man Talking

"You're supposed to be dead!" I proclaim to my best friend on my mother's special day. "Or at least *disappeared*."

"But I'm not," answers my formerly dead friend. "And what happened to your shirt?"

"Never mind my shirt," I bark as photos of my mother and Doorman Dave spill from my hand. "Why aren't you kaput?"

"Timmy, I just went on my vacation with my family. I told you about it. It was planned for the early part of this summer, but then with the whole strike and everything, we didn't know what we were gonna do."

"So what the heck *did* you do?" I cry.

"My mom asked the school if it was okay to go ahead with our vacation anyway. And since there was no actual instruction going on, they said it was fine."

"Wrong, wrong, wrong," I answer. "You're dead. Because if you weren't dead, you would have called."

"I *tried* to call you," answers Rollo. "Tons of times. But you never returned any of my messages."

YOU HAVE 54
— *RRRIBBITT* —
MESSAGES.

"Wrong again," I lecture Rollo. "Because I *always* return my messages! Messages from friends! Messages from clients! Even messages from faceless strangers!"

And as I say it, we are joined by another wedding guest.

Who is not a faceless stranger.

"Greetings, Rollo Tookus!" chirps Molly Moskins. "How was your vacation?"

"Fun!" says Rollo.

"Wait a minute!" I interrupt, and turn to Molly. "How did *you* know he was on vacation?"

"He told me about it before he left," she answers.

"Told you about it?" I cry. "And you never thought to mention it during the entire course of our felony investigation?"

"It didn't seem important," says Molly.

"Not important to mention that in a search for Rollo Tookus you knew where Rollo Tookus was?!"

"Well, when you put it that way," answers Molly.

"ARRRRGHHH," I cry, throwing the rest of the photos of my mother and Doorman Dave into the air.

"What's wrong?" asks Molly, picking up the photos.

"What's *wrong*, Molly Moskins, is that I *already solved* the case of Rollo's demise. He was kidnapped by a confederacy of dunces! A conspiracy of fools! And if there is one immutable principle in life, *it is that Timmy Failure is never wrong.*"

"Oh," says Molly. "So now what?"

I think fast.

"THE ROTUND BOY IN FRONT OF YOU IS A GHOST!" I shout triumphantly. *"And I will pass my hand through him as proof!"*

So I pass my arm through Rollo.

And it pokes him in the belly.

And just as I poke him, I am seized by another arm.

This one quite real.

CHAPTER 44
Down Goes Failure

It is the long arm of Merry Nightmare Before Christmas.

And I am once again being dragged through the air.

"We have to hurry!" she shouts. "It's the ring bearer's turn to walk down the aisle."

"But that can't be!" I cry. "You told my mom that you caught me doing detective work! That you saw me in my office!"

We enter the front doors of the church and stand in a small room cocooned by candles and flowers.

"So I'm grounded!" I continue. "Sent home! Kaput!"

And I see farther inside the church, through glass doors, a sea of strangers, staring back at me.

And as I stare, Merry kneels in her satin dress and grabs me by the padded shoulders of my tuxedo.

"I didn't tell her a thing," she answers as the church organ begins the wedding march. And I stare at my cousin.

"But . . . why not?" I ask.

"Because," she whispers into my ear, *"I*

always wanted to be a spy when I was a kid."

"I *knew* you were an international spy!" I cry.

And as she pulls me with one arm into her, I hear the rustle of satin and smell the fragrance of her hair.

"But my mom said it was stupid," she continues. "And not something a little girl should dream about."

And I see down to the far end of the aisle, where the priest motions with his hand for me to come forward.

"And so I love that you want to be a detective," whispers Merry as the swelling chords of the church organ swirl around us.

"But I *am* a detective!" I protest. "Right now. The world's *greatest* detective."

"I know," says Merry, standing and taking me by the hand. "I love that too."

"And I do too," interrupts Larry the Doomsdame, grabbing me by the other hand. "But if you don't hurry your big butt down the aisle, I will push you into a bed of roses."

"Go on," says Merry, handing me a soft satin pillow topped by a ring.

But I can't go on.

Because behind the floral arrangements, I see my polar bear, pale-faced and queasy.

"His bow tie is too tight!" I cry. "Who tied that thing? He's scared! He needs medical attention!"

"Go, Timmy, go!" says Larry, kneeing me in the rear end.

And as she does, I see my bear.

Wobble from side to side.

Eyes flickering closed.

His thunderous girth faltering, fainting, falling with the grace of an ancient redwood.

Onto a bed of floral arrangements.

And beyond him, my mother.

Dressed like I have never seen her before. Hazy and unreal. Like the ghost of Rollo Tookus.

"Go, sweetie, go," says my mother. "They're waiting for you at the altar."

And so I turn back to the altar. And see Doorman Dave. And the priest. And faceless guests. And Merry and Larry. And a downed bear.

And I look back at my mother, her white dress now gray. The candles around us dimming.

And the top of my head feels warm and prickly.

And my left knee buckles.

And then my right.

And one by one the candles flicker and go out.

As Merry and Larry grab for me.

The great Timmy Failure.

Falling with the grace of an ancient redwood.

CHAPTER
45

Just One More Thing

So I fainted.

Like all great men do in times of stress.

And as a result, I do not know what happened at the ceremony.

Though I'm told they got married.

But I didn't see it.

So there is no proof.

And you didn't see any of this, either.

In case anyone asks.

Especially your mother.

So please put the book down.

Because it's over.

Seriously.

It's over.

You never listen, do you?

Associate's Note:
From the Desk of
Molly Moskins

♥ ♥ ♥

Hi. This is me. Molly Moskins.

With a bigalicious confession.

And that is that *I'm* the person who stole this manuscript and gave it to booksellers and libraries.

I grabbed it when Timmy was talking to that crane operator at Home Despot.

♥ ♥ ♥

THIS MOMENT RIGHT HERE ←

And I did it because **TIMMY FAILURE IS A FANTASTICAL BRILLIANT GENIUS AND THE WHOLE WORLD NEEDS TO KNOW IT.**

And one more thing.

The name Timmy pulled out of that hat on our last day in the garden shed was:

Rollo Tookus

I guess the hat was only supposed to contain the names of evil suspects. But I didn't know that. So I filled it with the names of everyone I could think of.

Including Santa Claus, my cat Señor Burrito, and Barney the Dinosaur.

BUT I DIDN'T *DO* ANYTHING.

So if you're a fan of great detective novels, like me, and you need to know exactly what happened and who did what to whom and when, here are all the details:

1) The killer of Rollo was Rollo.
2) Rollo's not dead.
3) Yay! (because Rollo's not dead); and
4) I love you all.